To families everywhere who have made my books a part of
their children's lives. I am honored and words
cannot suffice. Thank you.
– KW

For Dylan
– JC

SIMON AND SCHUSTER
First published in Great Britain in 2009 by Simon and Schuster UK Ltd
1st Floor, 222 Gray's Inn Road, London, WC1X 8HB
A CBS Company

Originally published in 2009 by Margaret K. McElderry Books,
an imprint of Simon and Schuster Children's Publishing Division, New York

A CIP catalogue record for this book is available from the British Library upon request

ISBN: 978 1 84738 618 2 (PB)

Printed in China

1 3 5 7 9 10 8 6 4 2

Don't Be Afraid,
Little Pip

Karma Wilson illustrated by Jane Chapman

SIMON AND SCHUSTER

London   New York   Sydney

FLIP, FLAP, FLIP, FLAP!

Mummy and Daddy waddled up.
"It's your big day, Pip," said Daddy.
"Are you excited?"

"Soon you will be swimming with
all the other youngsters," said Mummy.

"But I'm a bird," frowned Pip,
"and birds fly."
"Don't be afraid, Little Pip," smiled Mummy.
"Penguins don't fly, we swim.
That's what makes us special."

Pip's parents sang . . .

"Into the water, under the sea
that's the best place for a penguin to be.
Flapping our wings and swishing on by.
Penguins can swim, so why should we fly?"

Pip didn't sing along.

"I still just want to fly,"
she whispered.

Soon all the young penguins were gathered at the shore. Their teacher, Mr Tucks, said, "Do not wander, younglings. Swimming is an art and you must learn properly."

A penguin sidled up to Pip.
"I can't wait! Can you?" she squeaked.
"Hi! I'm Merry. What's your name?"

Pip mumbled her name.

"Hello, Pip," Merry gushed. "Swimming!
This will be the best day of our lives!
Are you excited?"

Pip shook her head. "It's a bit scary.
What's under there, in the dark?"

"Oh, all sorts of wonderful things," said Merry,
"like a huge octopus, coral forests and giant
sea plants."

Pip shivered. "That doesn't help."

"We are penguins," said Merry,
"and all penguins swim."

"We are birds," said Pip.
"Shouldn't birds fly?"

Merry laughed. "Not penguin birds, silly."

Mr Tucks called out,
"Line up one by one.
It's time to begin."

In all the excitement, Little Pip slipped away.
"No swimming for me," she said.

FLAP, FLAP, SLAP!

I can learn to fly, thought Pip.
I just need some help.

Ahead, Pip saw a Snow Petrel.

"She can help!" cried Pip, racing towards the big bird.

"Hello!" said Pip. "I want to fly.
Can you help me?"

"You look like a penguin to me," said
the petrel, "and penguins don't fly."

Pip pointed to her feathers.
"I have wings," she said.
"I am a bird, too, so I can fly."

"Well, that's true," said the petrel.
"Maybe you *can* fly."

And she sang . . .
"*Pick up your feet, run down the shore.*
Flap your wings and flap some more.
Lift up your beak, look to the sky.
Take a leap and FLY, FLY, FLY!"

"Thank you," said Pip.

Pip ran.

Pip flapped.

She leaped and . . .

Pip flapped some more.

PLOP!

Pip fell.
Her beak was full of sand.

"Why do I even have wings?"
she sighed.

Pip waddled on until she came to another bird. This one was black and white – just like a penguin.

But it wasn't a penguin. It was a Giant Albatross.

"Hello!" said Pip.
"Can you help me?
I want to fly."

"And I want to swim in the ocean," chuckled the
albatross. "But I cannot, no more than penguins can fly."

"But, look, I have black wings, just like
yours," said Pip.

"Well, you are determined, I'll give you
that," said the albatross.
And he sang . . .
"*Stand on a ledge by the edge of the sea.*
Let your feathers set you free.
Lift your wings and spread them wide.
Jump into the breeze and away you'll glide!"

"Thank you," said Pip.

Pip found a ledge.

Pip climbed.

Pip spread her wings.

Pip jumped and . . .

"What are you doing, Pip?" said Merry.
"I wanted to fly," said Pip.
"Well, you're in the water so you'd better swim now," laughed Merry.
"Take a deep breath, kick your feet, and flap your wings. It's easy!
I'll help you."

Merry gave Pip a gentle nudge back into the waves.

Pip held her breath.

Pip kicked.

Pip flapped and . . .

Pip SWAM!

Deep under the water into the dark blue sea went Pip.
Whooosh! Whiiiish! Wheeeeee!
She swooped past a huge octopus, beautiful
coral reefs and giant sea plants.
She saw schools of fish as bright as
a rainbow in the sky.

Pip came up for air.
"Thank you, Merry!" she cried.
"I'm flying after all! Swimming is just
like flying – but under the sea!"

Darting and dashing, splishing and splashing through the waves, Pip and Merry swam together . . .

all the way back to shore.

When Mummy saw Pip she smiled.
"Little Pip, you can swim!" said Daddy.

They all snuggled
together and Pip sang . . .
"Into the water, under the sea
that's the best place for a penguin to be.
Flapping our wings and swishing on by.
Now I can swim and now I can fly!"